SUNIA SHORT STORIES COLLECTION

SUNIA BASU

Village Boy Turn To London Hero

His Name is Rocky he lives with his uncle and his uncle call him Rock. Someone offers his uncle money to send rocky to London airport they collect Rocky from there. They take Rocky as child labor because if they take from India then just give food and give some money in hands. They give visa and passport to go there and hid uncle get good money for it. Rocky 8 years old boy and he play flute very well. After his mom and dad dead his uncle has seen him. Now his uncle takes him to London and leaves him at the airport not see if they come and collect Rocky or not. He just goes in his own way. It is a story of a village boy how he became a London Hero.

Rocky see here and there but not see his uncle over there then he comes out from the airport. Does one taxi driver ask him from where you come? He says from India. Who comes with you? He says my uncle but now I can't see it. He ok, comes with me. He gives Rocky a work in a car garage. He works there and in break time he plays the flute. His dreams he wants to become a flute master. One day at break time his boss says he washes my car carefully. He takes a water pipe and starts washing the car with dancing. Other workers take a video on mobile and give it to on Facebook. In this way, Rocky life going on but he was not happy there. What Rocky like there is the fun of car garage?

One day in break time he playing the flute and that one customer comes there he listens to his flute and him with him. Rocky thinking now my life will changes and he now gives full time to flute and also learning English to perform better. After a few months later he performs on stage and takes the medal for it. In a few performs his name and photos come on newspaper and magazines. He earning good money performs flute on stage. He did not know when he became a London Hero. He just touches all people heart by playing

Flute. He just misses his country and his village so much. He does not have that much money to come back to India. Just pray for Rocky that he can come back to India some day.

------------------ END ------------------

Three Mischievous Guys

Three Friends decide to go for cycle rider and keep the close look of that town. They are name is Ricky, Dicky, and Bicky. Guys start there cycle rider but not say to their mom and dad. After some time they search here and there but not get it. Guys are 7, 8 and 9 years old. Guys go on there on way. Sing a song with cycle rider and also make fun, do not thinking that mom and dad search us. Before going for a ride they take heavy breakfast so do not worry about food.
They ride through railway track and in garbage area were whole city garbage fall. Now ride from the side of the river and stop there. Playing with river water and also wash face in river water. There they show one man how to sell peanut but they do have money to buy it. After that guys think to make fool him and take peanuts. At that time one man comes to buy peanut and guys fool him for peanut. He pays for them and goes from there.
Now guys ride from someone garden where they show guava tree stop there but the tree is so high they can't get a hand on it. Dicky tries to climb to that tree and others are watch if someone coming or not. Dicky takes three guavas and comes down. After that guy rubs that guava in their clothes and has it. After that start ride again after half an hour's ride guys think for fun in park but again they do not have an entry fee to in there.
Guys go back sides of that park were they see one gate that has broken. Guys go in from there and play on there but they do not lock there cycles it just lying in the broken gate. When guys come back to

that broken gate cycles are not there. Guys show the thief and follow them to get back there cycles. At that thief get hit to a light post and fall down. Guys caught him and hand over to police. Its evening time, now guys feel hungry they want to eat something but no money what to do guys thinking?
At that time Bicky show someone pocket 100 rupees note fall down he just pick it up and give sweet shop guy for some foods. Take that food and have it. Now take the way home because it winters time guys not take their jackets with them to take away to home. In the way, guys change their mind and say speedy up ride so we do not get cold. Therein way they see one cake shop stop there and watch what is happening there? That time one lady take the hot chocolate cake in one packet 6 cakes and other one 3 cakes guy's see that.
Lady forgot to take 3 cakes packets, Bicky see that he pick that packet and run to hand over this packet to that lady but she was gone from there. Guy's taken that cake and eats it. At that shop, watch Shaw at 10.00 PM. Ricky says now we should go home it is too late but not go in from the front door. Go from back door and entry to their bedroom. When their mom came they are in their own room. Guys are from the same family and cycle ride ends here.
-------------------- THE END ------------------

Confused Guy

He is a 21-year-old and his name is Bobby Wilson. When I am in London, I meet him there. He stands in front of my flat. I call him bro because he is younger than me. He is so confused he can't make any decisions, so his friends call him Confuse. Bobby has a girlfriend but he can't tell her he loves her because of confusion whether she loves me or not. He can take a decision about his life and what he wants to become? Bobby studies at Cambridge University in London, where his friends also call him confused. Nobody knows him by his real name. Everyone knows the confusion about him at university but Bobby is helpless. He can't come out of it. Bobby's girlfriend also shouts at him for this reason.

Bobby is from a rich family and he is the only son of their parents, so they do not stop bobby for anything. His dad says enjoy your life in your own way, but Bobby does not make a decision about what to do. Will he go for a drive with his girlfriend or go with friends to a club for a party? Every time bobby thinks he is totally confused, then bobby plays guitar to cool down, but there is also confusion about what to play and what not to play? Bobby does not get relief from confusion. He starts riding his bike in the middle of the road. His friends said, What happened? Bobby thinking I should go forward or not? His friends say stop thinking too much, let go on the way, bobby life going on this way.

girlfriend. But Bobby is confused again about what to do or not to ask his girlfriend. His girlfriend says let go it will be fun. Bobby says, but where do we stay? His friend says in a haunted house too scared bobby. You all lied to me. Tell me the truth. His friends said he was in the guest house for 4 days. They started their drive. After sometime, Bobby asks if we are in the right way? His friends say yes, confused, just come out of your confusion otherwise our fun will turn to a sad moment. After a few hours, they reach the guest house again. Bobby says it was that guest house that we wanted to go to? They answered again, Yes, confused. Now can we go in? Bobby says yes, we will.

In the evening, Bobby's friends open a beer bottle. That time, Bobby asked, was this a beer or colored water? Now his friends are laughing and saying yes, it is a beer. You try it on your own. At that time, wind blows outside and Bobby says it is wind or is it a ghost coming here? His friends say yes, a ghost comes to catch you confused. Bobby's girlfriend closes the guest house door and comes back to the seat. Does Bobby say we all here then who is in the kitchen? His friends say you go and see it. After that, Bobby goes there and the window is open, so the wind blows sound coming nothing else. He shuts the window and comes back. Bobby's friends say what to do with this confused? For bobby, they come in 2 days. Now his friends decide not to take bobby anywhere with them. Bobby's girlfriend also left him because of this confusion, but still he did not come out of it. Confusion not leave bobby still now.

------------------ THE END ----------------

Bike Rider

This story is all about a bike rider who's age is 40 or 45. He is from rice his dress up and his bike say that. That road is outside of the school. The school name is Assembly of God Church Schools. I studied there that time when this happened. Our school is over at 2:00 PM and that time rushes on that road, so cars and bikes go slow at that time. From our school to home is just 20 minutes' distance, so i go home by walking. One day when school is over, I make my way to home. At that time, from my back, one bike rider comes and goes with my leg finger. I shouted, you can't see, but he had just gone in his own way. His was very roughly riding what would happen no one knew.

Then he hit a lamp post and fell down, but his speed did not go slow. Just stand up and ride again. Everyone is scared. What will he do next? He can't control his bike properly but still not slow his speed. He was now going forward and one truck came from there. He just went from under that truck. People are saying what he is doing, is he mad or what? Now he hits the tea shop side where some people sit and drink tea. They shout what you are doing, are you mad and bit

him. He still has not changed his mind. He goes on his own way. He is
rich, so he thinks he can do anything and stop people mouth's giving
money. On that road, not only common people was there but school
boys and girls were there.
He now took a turn to the left where on the right side a high drain
was there. A school boy 6 or 7 years old goes from that side.
Suddenly, he goes to the right and hits that boy. He felt on high drain
but that bike rider did not see back to see what happen to the boy.
Some people came there to take him out from high drain and send to
hospital. A bike rider is a heartless person with no sympathy for
children or anyone. We all never know what will happen to that child.
Is he still alive or not?
----------------------------THE END----------------------------

Dr. Lady Hitler

It is a story of a lady doctor. Her real name is Dr. Jojo, but nobody
knows her in her real name. All the staff know her as Jungle cat or
jiddi. She did not like mama's boy how do everything as his mother's
say. If they come in front of her to propose, then see bit them this
way that their bones gone dust like sand. Some boys are if someone
try to propose with red rose. When he went forward to propose,
Rose felt down only the stick in his hand. Boys are said rose also
scared to go in jungle cat hand. She has 3 elder brothers. They also
call her house cat because she can't take lunch or dinner without fish.
She does not much like chicken and mutton.
Her parents decide to give her marriage. So, her father's friend's son
jay meet her at home. Both parents want them to go out for a drive
or movie, so they can spend time with each other. Next day, Jay called
her and said to come to the shopping mall for coffee. She went to
the mall and met him. Then they go to drink coffee. She said give an

order and he called his mom. He asked his mom which coffee he should take Cappuccino, Espresso or Macchiato. He did not ask his girlfriend what to take. She got angry and went on without saying anything to him. If he was not her dad's friend's son, then she would break his bones, like sand. She comes home and says her dad she will not marry a mama's boy. If he comes in front of me again, then i will bite him like anything else. No one can control her. If she is angry, then her head goes hot. She did not care about anyone that time. She didn't even take her parents'word.

They have got invitation cards for the party. Her parents are scared of her. What does she do there? She can't tolerate mama's boys and bad jokes. Her mom says wears a saree but she's not comfortable with sarees, so she wears western dresses. After reaching the party, she heard someone say Dr. Jiddi came see there. After that, she saw that some girls had time passed with one boy. She asked her friend how he was? She answered my best friend Ajay and he is an business magnets. After sometime, Ajay saw her and said to his friends, who is she? They answered Dr. Jiddi or jungle cat or lady hitler. You can call her by any name, but no one calls her by her real name. What is her real name Ajay asked friends? They say jojo. Do not go there. She will fire on you and your bones become sand. Ajay says this rose will be in our garden.

Ajay, goes forward and proposes to her. Ajay, say will you marry me? She said what? Ajay Yes I mean it. Will you be my forever? Suddenly, announced to dance there. Ajay offers her to dance. She accepted it. Now they are all dancing there with romantic songs. When dancing she says, Ajay I hate mama's boy". He says you want to say i am a mama's boy? She said I did not talk about you. She asked," Why do you want to marry me? You have not heard of me. Ajay says I know everything about you. I still want to marry you because this jungle rose will be in our garden, my jungle cat. Then they got married and

went for their honeymoon. Lady Hatler does not change after married also. She is in her own way.
-----------------------------THE END-----------------------------

Cute Tomato

The story started with cute tomato. He live with his uncle and there are very poor. His uncle can't give food daily. He is 5 years old boy. His mom and dad are death when he is 6 months old. His uncle take him to childern park, where many gather with their child. In left side of park on bench one rich man siting. Tomato uncle tell him go to your dad and stay with him. Do not leave him along. He go there and call him dad. He asked how is your dad? Tomato say you. He say me, tomato say yes you. Then people gather there say why you want to leave your boy along? He say he is not my boy. Tomato he my dad. Than people you take him with you or we call police. He say no do not call police i will take care of him. He take tomato with his car, go to his home. His mom and dad say how is he? Tomato answer he is my dad and i am tomato his son.
Next morning he take him to his girlfriend house. Tomato call her mom. His girlfriend say what i am your mom how say you that? Tomato answer my dad. He say to his girlfriend i do not understand from where he come for. He not leave me along what shall i do not understand. His girlfriend say send him to bodine school, so you get relief for him. He take him to bodine school leave him there. Next day call from bodine school you take him from here he is too naughty not give other to study and also fight with them. You take him from here as soon as possible. He go to bodine school and take him back. He take tomato to that childern park and sit on bench. Tomato sleep there and he leave tomato their. He then come back to home. Suddenly he see that rain coming, so he run back and take tomato

back home. Next day morning after breakfast over. He take tomato to shopping mall to buy dress for him. After shopping over they go to hotel for lunch. There he call his girlfriend also for lunch. His girlfriend say why you take him here? No other option left for me, so will you be his mom? She say ok, i will be. Then they married and happly leave with cute tomato. He has touch their heart.

--------------------------------THE END----------------------------------

Rosevilla Banglow

This story is about Rosevilla Banglow, which is in Digha, but from Digha's main city, 5 km away. It is in west Mandarmani Digha. My friends are planning to go to Mandarmani and stay in Rosevilla Banglow. We started our journey by car. We are going with 3 boys and 3 girls to Mandarmani Digha. Their names are Rikey, Bikey, Dikey and the girls' names are Pinkey, Rinkey and me Sunia. We just enjoy our driving with songs. We take our lunch at a roadside hotel and again start driving. In the car, singing and joking. There were 2 couples and they will be married soon. So, love jokes are also happening in cars with singing and dance. Suddenly, my friend stops in the road. On that road no vehicle is shown. Only we are their, they sing and dance on the road. Its like we are all in a festival mood.

We drive again. When we take the road to Rosevilla banglow, then we show in roadside it written stop here and go back. We do not understand written notes. We are going forward to Rosevilla. It is the evening. No light posts on that road, we see from our mobile torch. Then we heard some sound coming, do not go there." If you go then no body will be alive. We were scared. That time, it was like somebody took our car into control but we couldn't see anyone there. Finally, we reached Rosevilla Banglow and it was so beautiful, we took photos and video of it. Then we went inside and asked

someone if there was? No answer came from there. Then my friend Dikey opened the fridge and saw the full fridge was packed with food. Then Pinkey prepared coffee for everyone and I taken some biscuits for everyone. After drinking coffee, we all go to refresh ourselves. When we came down i got want diary of Rose. Its written she is not alive now. She died 5 years ago and now in Rosevilla, Rose's ghost will stay and she will not leave anyone. How come to stay at Rosevilla? Suddenly, a voice coming did not touch my diary. Just leave here, otherwise I will kill all of you. Rikey said in the morning we would go from here. She answered not in the morning, just leave now from here. Then we got our luggage and went out of Rosevilla and ran to our car. She burned our car. We ran from there. She says if you all want to be alive, then run how fast you can. Suddenly, we couldn't see Pinkey over there. We were just scared and shouted her name, but no answer came. We go forward and see she kill her. Then we run faster and we feel that someone is taking a deep breath. Then we can't see Rikey. She kills him also. We decided that we should not go along. We should be in a group, then only we can be alive.
After a sometime, Dikey said" I have to go to the toilet now. We say do not go far away. He also just vanished in front of our eyes. We are afraid now but still running to be alive. Then we see Rinkey, also not found. Still, we go forward hoping for the best. Then we see Dikey and Rinkey's dead bodies in front of our eyes. Bikey and I just prayed that the sun would come out and we would be saved. Suddenly, I couldn't see Bikey anywhere there. I just went forward and saw Bikey's death body was theirs. On the side of that road was written the way to Rosevilla. Suddenly, the sun came out but i lost all my friends there. I take the lift from the car to go back home, but I will never forget this journey to Mandarmani Digha.
-------------------------------THE END-----------------------------

Pizza Delivery Boy

This story is about a pizza delivery boy. His name is Raju and he is 21 years old boy. Raju got a call from apartment Rojina, flat no.13. That flat is on the 13th floor. He went to that apartment, rojina and he went to the lift for pizza delivery to the 13th floor at flat no.13. Raju says mam pizza for you. She said, come in. The door is open. He goes into the room but it is dark. No light is there. He asked where are you mam? I do not see you mam, it is too dark. She answered, dark for that you are hear me. Raju, what are you talking about? She answered yes, it was true. He got on his mobile torch and tried to look at it. He saw a shadow pass away. He was scared.
He asked mam where I kept the pizza? She answered on the table. He kept pizza on the table and asked for a pizza payment, mam. She answered, wait for that still morning. Raju answered I can't wait until morning. I have to give the pizza somewhere else. Please give me payment now. She said just wait na" in an angry tone. Suddenly, he saw a dim light on in that room. He did not turn on any switches, but then also dim light on their. He was thinking, what is happening here? He again asked to mam please give me pizza payment. I am getting late. Then he turned back and saw someone eating that pizza. He only saw the shadow of her. He was just scared and trying to go out from there but door is shurt down.
He shouted for help. Please somebody help me get out of here, but no answer comes from outside. He started praying to god when the sun came out. After a few hours, light came out from under the door of that room. He pulled the door from inside and it opened. He saw the pizza payment on the floor. Raju picked up that money and ran to the lift, but the lift did not stop at the 13th floor. He was so scared, he just ran from the stairs from the 13th floor to the ground floor. The watchman asked, why are you so scared? He answered on the 13th

floor of flat no.13 to go for pizza delivery. The watchman said that on the 13th floor, nobody stayed on that floor because it was fully haunted. He says you are still alive. That is good news. Raju answered, then who is she? The watchman answers that it is Rojina's ghost, who died 5 years ago. Then Raju took his bike and went from there.

-----------------------------------THE

END--------------------------------------

Deadly Drive Car

This belongs to guys who deadly drive car. Do not worry about if anyone comes in front of the car what will happen. The guys names are Peter, John and Sunny. One day they plan to go for a deadly drive in a car. As their plan, Peter would collect the car from the show room. Peter went there and rejected a car for a free drive. That shop boss does not know that they are taking a car for a deadly drive. Peter took the go to that spot where his friends were waiting. His friends get into a car and the deadly driving starts. The first car goes from the market area where people buy fruit and vegetables. In that market, some shops are broken and some people are injured, but they do not stop the car because they lose control of the car. John said I would drive now. He takes control of the car but the crowd shouts at them. They get scared and go out from there.

After a few minutes later, they came in front of a bridge. Now sunny plan to go over the bridge by car. The bridge is small and it can't take heavy loads. It's written on the side of that bridge. Only a bicycle or bike can go over it but they do not care about the notice. They go over the bridge. When the car came to the bridge, it broke in the middle. Now their car is half in the air and half on bridges. Sunny tried to go forward but he felt to do that. His two friends came out of the car and pushed the car from behind. Then they cross the bridge before it fully broken. Peter said, how will we go back fully broken? John said the other way we go back. Do not bore me. Just enjoy the deadly drive.

Then their car goes over the garbage area. The car just jumps there but they do not stop. There was one women collecting paper from there. Their car hit that woman's leg, she felt down and shouted that her leg was broken. Catch the car guys. They speed up their car and hit a lamp post. Now their car doors are broken. The car goes without a door. Now hits to standing police van and run car from their. Police follow them to catch them. They take a short cut to get relief from the police. Their car now goes from the bamboo garden where there are lie down there. They take the car over the bamboo and there hits to bamboo plant over there. Now their car top gone but they do not stop still.

Now they go from sea to beach side. People crowd over their but they go through it. People were running here and there. What don't they understand? Someone called police their. When they hear police coming, then they go from there. Now they plan to bring some food. They go to a hotel for lunch. After over lunch, they take their bill and add it to the bill, then go there. Then they hit an old house there nobody leave their. Now their car head light also gone. Finally, they took the way to home but they did not see a police van come in their way. Again, they hit the police van. Now they do not get time to run back and be arrested.

----------------------------THE END----------------------------

Burning Girl

This story is about a village girl and she comes for a home job for 24 hours. She is a 13-year-old girl and her name is Puja. The family bought her from the village. They are rice. There are 12 members in the family. The family head member's name is Abir Ghosh and his wife's name is Anita Ghosh. They have 3 sons' names are Abhishek's elder son and his wife Anjali. They have one boy and one girl. Their names are Roni and Remi. Their ages are Roni 8 years old and Remi 6 years old. Abir's second son's name is Abhijeet and his wife's name is Anushila. They have 2 girls and their names are Mili and Juli. They are both 6 years old. Abir's little son's name is Abinash and his wife's name is Anushka. They have one boy and one girl. Their son's name is Boni and the girl's name is Bunny. Their ages are Bunny is 6 years old and Boni is 4 years old. They have their own bakery, photo studio, wooden shop and iron shop. They have also cooked. She comes only once in the morning. We call it Abir Dadu(That means grandfather). The bakery and house are in his name.

One day, the morning when he read the newspaper at that time, puja was there. She gives water to money plant and other plants. In the newspaper onsite, it was written that one girl burned her body on fire. Puja heard that and asked him how she burned herself. Does it not give a burning sensation in the body? He answers that you just forget it and pay attention to your work. This news roamed in her mind and she thought I should do this one day. After lunch, she took the newspaper and read those lines again. She wanted to know how she burned herself. Puja saw there it was written that there was a sprawl of kerosene oil on her body. She goes to the terrace to give wet clothes to dry in sunlight. There she saw a kerosene oil jar. She thought that I should also try this.

After a few minutes, we saw black smoke coming towards our house. Then I heard someone shouting," Help me, please, I do not want to die. Puja ran up the stairs to the 1st floor. Their terrace is on the 3th floor. From there she runs and comes down to the 1st floor. Anjali covered her in a blanket and the fire stopped. They called an ambulance and took her to the hospital. When they take her to an

ambulance, that time they say you told the police you did it on your own. We do not force you to do that. Then she was senseless. When that sense came back, the police asked her to say it. Why do you do this? Does anyone force you to do that? She answered, no I will do it on my own. They do not force me to do so. Next morning she died.
------------------------------THE END----------------------------

Haunted House

I live with my parents in a private house on rent. We stayed on the 1st floor of that private house. After a few days, we realize that someone lives with us and it's a shadow ghost. In that house on the 2nd floor, our landlord was staying. They face some problems also but, not say to anyone. They also feel someone are their. So they call Mandir pujari their and he just runs from there. Then they come down and say I can't do anything. It's a ghost problem. We all realize that someone goes up and down the stairs at night at 2:30 to 3:00 AM. Sometimes, in the evening, people also see shadows pass away. Even in the afternoon at 2:00 PM, I also shaw her pass from my side when i surfing on my PC. She is a 19 or 20-year-old girl showing here. We see only shadows moving here and there. It's a young lady's shadow we see here, so i am scared. What to do now?
In the afternoon, at 2:30 PM, I was watching a movie on TV and suddenly I saw a shadow pass away in front of the TV. I was just scared and thinking what was happening in this house? She passed in front of the kitchen. Our cook gets scared seeing this. She was preparing food when she saw her pass away from in front of the kitchen. She was steal there for a few mins. At night, after dinner, when I went to bed i feeling that someone was sitting on my bed at my headside. I was scared and taking god's name to get relive from it. She started shaking my bed, her shadow was showing on the walls. I

wouldn't be able to run away from here. She captured the room fully. In that room my mom is also there. She was sleeping at that time and she was bedded patient.

In the early morning, she passes away in front of the fridge and dressing table. It's like someone opening a fridge and closing it. With this scare, how can we live here, we thinking? After that, in the evening when I am watching TV, I hear someone say hello but, I can't see anyone behind me.She wants to say something to us, by doing this things, but we do not understand what she wants to say? . I was scared. Then we saw her shadow was a young girl. We decide we should leave the house forever because she want to take revenge to owner of the house. Finally, we took the decision to shift from there.

--THE
END--

Triangular Love Story

It is the story of three guys. They love one girl. Guys do not know who loves whom? They study in the 12th standard in our school and it is a convent school. The true story happens in our school outside gate for these our principal declared three days holiday's. Guys make fun with her share Tiffin and also give gift to her. She accepts it as a friendship gift. Guys are scared to say that they love her. The guys' names are Sonu, Monu and Ponu. The girl's name is Pooja and she is a good friend of this guys. One day when class is going on, Sonu throws paper pieces to Pooja and in that paper written I LOVE U. Pooja throw that paper to Sonu again and in that paper written in capital letter NO. Sonu get angry because he guesses it Monu whom she loves. In Tiffin's time, Sonu saw her. Pooja sees that and she goes with Monu to see what Sonu is doing now. Sonu is so jealous that he throws his Tiffin into the dustbin. Our school rules that you can speak in your own language at tiffin time. So, everyone speaks in his or her own language at school tiffin time. So pooja friends sing in Hindi to impress pooja but she does not care about that. She carried on with other friends.

After school is over, Sonu tries to give a lift to Pooja but he sees her going with Monu. Sonu now makes plans to take revenge on Monu. Next day, in Tiffin time Monu proposed pooja and she says" you are just my good friend nothing else. Sonu does not hear that he is in his own way. Monu now guesses it is Sonu that loves her love, so she tries to fool him. Sonu and Monu are so confused they make plans to take revenge on each other without knowing the truth. Ponu takes advantage of it. He now offers Pooja to go for a drive with him. Pooja says OK. Sonu or Monu nobody sees it. Next day, Pooja comes with Monu's Bike and Sonu sees that he then throws a stone at Monu, but it does not hit Monu. After some time, Sonu fell down in class. Everybody thought he was ill and the teacher sent him home, but he did not want to go home. Sonu's mind and heart couldn't take this, so he fell. Nobody knew that.

Next day, Sonu pushes Monu from behind and hides from him. After that, class started but Sonu couldn't give his mind to the lesson. He is jealous, he is only thinking about revenge, nothing else. After school over outside of school gate Sonu suddenly fire on Monu and Monu also fire on Sonu by pistol. In school, how? Nobody knows that? They lie down on the spot. Pooja, seeing this, ran from there and caught a taxi to go home. Ponu shouted Pooja wait do not go but she take her own way. Someone calls the police, they take them to hospital. Pooja was rusticated from school because the principal said it all happened to pooja. Next morning, we hear Sonu and Monu are dead. Just for confusion, they lost their lives. If they try to know the truth, then they will still be alive. This story teaches one thing do not make any decisions in confusion. The guys are from a rich family, so the case ends there. One question is still roaming in all minds how pistols come inside school?

------------------ THE END ------------------

Contents